For my dad, and for that pesky woodpecker
pecking the metal pole outside our house,
who inspired this book.

www.mascotbooks.com

POPPER AND FRIENDS: Popper Finds a New Home

For more information, please contact:

Mascot Books

620 Herndon Parkway #320

Herndon, VA 20170

info@mascotbooks.com

Library of Congress Control Number: 2021909496

CPSIA Code: PRT0621A

ISBN-13: 978-1-64543-992-9

Printed in the United States

POPPER AND FRIENDS

Popper
Finds a New Home

IL Ritchie

Illustrated by
Yulia Potts

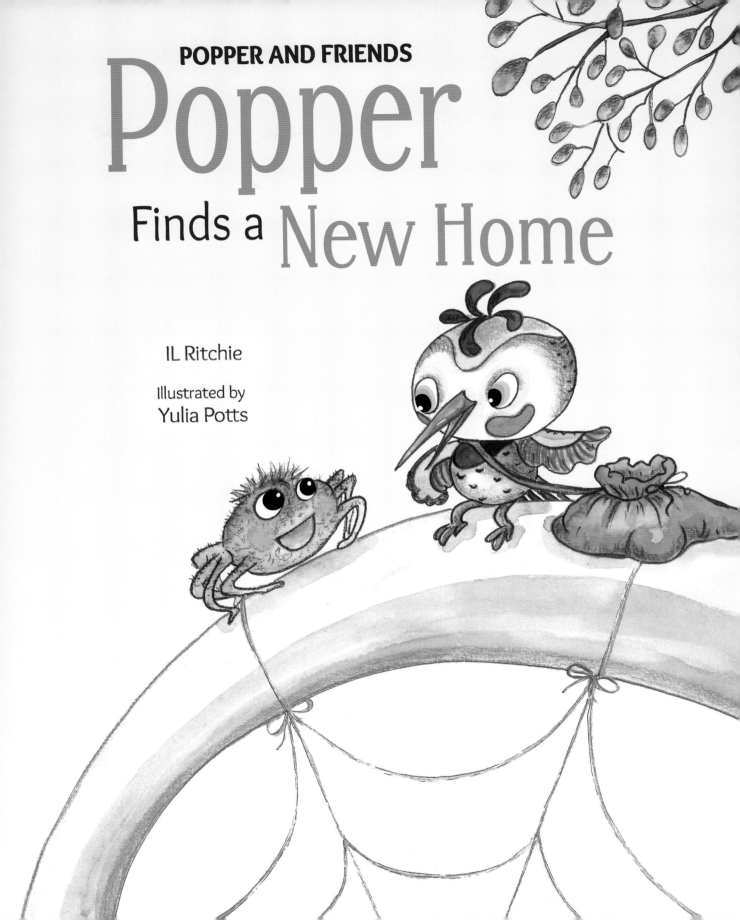

One bright and sunny morning, Popper the woodpecker woke up to find that he had grown too big for his bed! Popper was no longer a baby woodpecker.

"Mom and Dad, something's wrong with my bed!" Popper said.

"Don't worry, Popper," his mom said. "There's nothing wrong, you're just growing up!"

Popper realized it was time to leave his parents' house and find his own home, where there would be plenty of space for him. "I'm going to find a home of my own!" Popper told his parents cheerfully.

Popper's parents wished him well as he set off on his adventure.

First, Popper flew to the pond, where he saw Burton the bullfrog sitting on his lily pad.

"Hi Burton! I'm looking for a new house," Popper said.

"That's great, Popper, but woodpeckers don't live by water," Burton chuckled. "You'll need to find somewhere else to live."

Popper thanked Burton and flew off to continue his search.

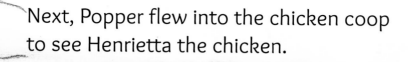

Next, Popper flew into the chicken coop to see Henrietta the chicken.

"Hi Henrietta! I'm looking for a new house," Popper said.

"I'm so proud of you, Popper, but woodpeckers don't live this low to the ground. You'll have to find something higher," Henrietta offered.

Next, Popper tried the windowsill of Farmer John's house. Farmer John and his family were eating breakfast when they saw Popper come to their window.

"Hi Popper!" Farmer John said to greet Popper.

"Hi John! I'm looking for a new house, and this windowsill seems like it might work," Popper said.

"I'm sorry, Popper, but the windowsill won't work. You need to find somewhere you can burrow, so that you can build your own house," Farmer John said.

Popper set off again, and this time he flew into Farmer John's barn. In the barn, Popper saw Herwin the owl. Popper squinted to see inside the dark barn.

"Whooooo's there?" asked Herwin.

"Herwin, it's me, Popper. I'm looking for a new house. I was thinking I could find somewhere to burrow in this barn," Popper said.

"I see," said Herwin. "Popper, you don't want to live inside a dark barn—you should find somewhere outside, where you can create your home in the fresh air."

Popper let out a heavy sigh. "I don't know if I'll ever find a new home," he said.

"Don't get discouraged, Popper. I'm sure you will find the perfect place!" Herwin said.

Next, Popper found a nearby streetlight. *Surely this could be my new house!* he thought. Popper began pecking at the streetlight, but it made an awful loud racket.

"Who's making all that noise?" asked Webster the spider.

"Hi, Webster. It's me, Popper. I'm trying to find a new house, and I thought this was going to work."

"Oh Popper, this streetlight is metal. You need to find wood to peck in order to build your house," Webster offered.

Popper was disappointed, but he thanked Webster as he headed off to continue his search.

Popper found a utility pole next, which he was convinced could be his new house. But when Popper landed on the pole, he realized Filbert the squirrel lived in a nest right next to where he wanted to build his new house!

"Hi Popper! What's going on?" Filbert asked.

"Hi Filbert. I've been flying around all day, looking for the perfect place to build my new house. I thought I had found it, but this won't work either," Popper said sadly. He was getting more concerned that he wouldn't be able to find the perfect home.

"Popper, when you left your parents' house this morning, weren't there other trees nearby?" asked Filbert. "Perhaps one of those trees would make a good home!"

"That's it!" Popper exclaimed. He couldn't believe he hadn't thought of that before. "Thanks, Filbert!"

Popper rushed back to the trees next to his parents' house. He looked around happily at the trees, so excited to finally have a place to build his new house! Everyone could hear Popper pecking, so they knew he had found his new home.

"We knew you could do it, son!" said Popper's dad as he proudly observed Popper's work.

"I'm so happy I found a home!" said Popper. "Now, I'll have plenty of space and can still see you anytime I want!"

The next day, everyone came by to see Popper
and wished him well in his new home.

The End

About the Author

IL Ritchie was born and raised in Northern California. Growing up, his dad talked about a woodpecker that made a racket when it pecked a nearby metal pole. Although it was likely a way to establish its territory and attract a mate, it seemed like this woodpecker was trying to burrow into the metal. Ritchie's dad joked that the woodpecker was giving itself an awful headache! Ritchie always thought that maybe the woodpecker was just communicating with its friends—and the idea for Popper was born.

About the Illustrator

Yulia Potts is an illustrator from the emerald hills of New Zealand. She and her family live the cottage life of the 1900s surrounded by alpacas, sheep, and other animals. She believes there is an extraordinary story to tell about every ordinary thing around us.

Visit Yulia online at www.myhoneyland.nz

myhoneyland_illustrations

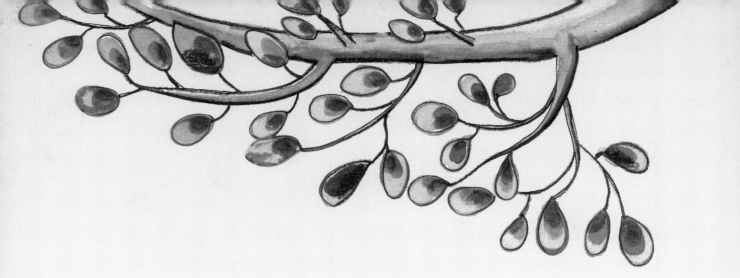